The Twelve Dancing Princesses

By The Brothers Grimm

Retold by Diane Muldrow
Illustrated by Fred Marvin

A GOLDEN BOOK • NEW YORK
Western Publishing Company, Inc., Racine, Wisconsin 53404

Come a little closer, and I will tell you about a
king who had twelve lively and beautiful daughters.

The princesses slept in the great hall of the castle,
their beds all in a row. "Good night, my daughters,"
their father said each night. Then he locked the door
behind him to keep his loved ones safe.

But each morning when the door was unlocked, what do you think the king found? Twelve pairs of dainty dancing shoes, worn through with holes. No one could say how this came to pass.

The king announced that any young man who could
discover where his daughters danced each night would
inherit the throne and win one of his daughters for a bride.
But whoever did not succeed within three days and nights
would be sent away from the kingdom forever.

One day a soldier coming home from the wars met an old woman who asked where he was going.

"I haven't decided," he replied, and added with a laugh, "unless it's to find where the king's daughters dance every night, and so become king."

The woman beckoned him closer. "That is not as difficult as it seems," she whispered. "Just don't drink anything the princesses may offer you. And take this cloak, for it will make you invisible to others."

"Thank you, dear woman," said the soldier. He went straight to the king's court, where he was welcomed with new clothes and a chamber off the great hall.

That evening the eldest princess appeared with a hot drink, saying, "Drink quickly, sir, for it will not stay warm for long!"

The soldier pretended to drink, but the liquid ran down into a sponge he had tied under his chin. Then he lay down and pretended to snore. The sisters laughed at this and said, "Sleep well, soldier!"

Bringing out elegant gowns, they then dressed themselves before the mirrors, arranged each other's hair, and whispered excitedly about the ball they would attend that night.

But the youngest daughter said, "I feel so strange tonight, as if something is hanging over us."

"Don't be a goose," replied the eldest. "I hardly needed to give that soldier a sleeping potion—the fool would have fallen asleep anyway."

When all were dressed and ready, they quieted themselves and peered closely at the soldier, who pretended to sleep.

The eldest princess then tapped her bed; it immediately sank into the earth. The twelve young women descended, one by one, into the opening, with the soldier behind them, invisible in his cloak. Halfway down, he stepped on the youngest daughter's dress.

"Who is pulling at my gown?" cried the frightened girl.

"Don't be silly," chided the eldest. "You have caught it on a nail."

At the bottom of the staircase stretched a long avenue of trees with leaves of sparkling silver.

Said the soldier to himself, "One of these leaves will be proof to the king that I followed his daughters." With that—*crack*—he broke off a twig.

The youngest daughter jumped at the sound. "What was that noise?" she cried, but her sisters only laughed.

The merry group turned onto another avenue, where
the leaves were gold, and then onto a third, where the
trees twinkled with diamonds. On each avenue the
soldier broke off twigs from the trees— *crack! crack!*—
causing the youngest to shake with fear.

The princesses arrived at the banks of a lake where twelve pretty boats floated, with a prince waiting in each one. The soldier was quick to follow the youngest princess into her boat.

"Our boat feels so much heavier today," remarked the prince. "I have to use all my strength to row across."

Across the water was a palace blazing with lights. Sweet music drifted through the open doorways.

There the soldier watched the princesses dance until three o'clock in the morning, when one of them said, "Oh, dear. I can dance no more—my shoes are worn through with holes."

"Mine, too. And mine," chimed in the others. And so it was time for the princes to ferry their ladies back across the lake. This time the soldier rode back with the eldest princess.

While the young ladies bid good night to their princes, the soldier quickly ran back to the palace, crawled into bed, and closed his eyes. The princesses slowly climbed the stairs and heard him snore so loudly that they said, "We are quite safe from him." They hung up their beautiful dresses and finally went to sleep.

Next morning the soldier told no one what he had
seen. He wanted to see the sparkling trees and the
palace again, so on the second and third nights, he
followed the princesses as before. On the third night
he took a golden cup as proof of his visit.

The soldier was summoned before the king the next day.
"How do my daughters wear out their dancing
shoes each night?" asked the king.

"Your Highness, they travel to an underground castle and dance with twelve princes until three o'clock in the morning," replied the soldier. He presented to the astonished king the three branches and the golden cup.

"Is this true?" roared the king. The daughters could
not deny it.

So the king said, "Soldier, which of my daughters will
you have for a wife?"

"I am no longer young," answered the soldier. "I will
marry your eldest daughter if she will have me."

The eldest realized that the soldier was not a fool, after all, and would be the future king. For the first time she smiled at the soldier. Holding out her hand, she said, "Yes, I will."

Soon there was a large wedding. The king forgave his naughty daughters, and so the day was a happy one. The lovely bride and her sisters danced until . . . yes, my dears, three o'clock in the morning.